ROBERTO AND THE MAGICAL FOUNTAIN

DONNA REID VANN

Roberto and the Magical Fountain

ILLUSTRATIONS BY
John Haysom

A LION PICTURE STORY
Oxford · Batavia · Sydney

In the sunny city of Barcelona, Spain, there lived a boy whose name was Roberto. The children on his street had nicknamed him "Roberto of the Roses". This was because on his face he had a birthmark which looked like three red roses.

This mark had been there ever since Roberto was born. Nothing could hide it; nothing could take it away.

"Roberto of the Roses!
Roberto of the Roses!"

The shouts of the other children reached his ears each day as he walked down the street. He paid little attention to the teasing. His father loved him; his mother loved him, and his sister Laia thought him the most wonderful of older brothers.

Roberto was happy enough, in his life in the bustling city. From the window of his tiny bedroom he could glimpse the glittering green sea. Often he would wander shoulder-to-shoulder with the crowds on the broad boulevard, always stopping near the stalls hung with cages of parakeets for sale.

Roberto felt sorry for the caged birds. He would touch his finger to the door of a cage, longing to fling it open and watch the parakeet soar to the heavens. He did not dare really to set the bird free. The stall-keeper would yell at him and demand money, and Roberto had none. But since ideas cost nothing, he would let the bird go free in his thoughts. In his mind he watched as it flew upward toward the sun.

Near the boulevard were many fine shops, but he never dared to enter them. The sunny street was the proper place for such a one as Roberto of the Roses, a boy who was different.

One day, however, there arose in Roberto's heart the longing for something more.

"I am not happy," he thought, though he did not know why.

He decided to do something he had never done before. He walked up the boulevard and boldly went into the largest department store in Barcelona.

Roberto stood stock-still. He had never seen such a magnificent place. There were crowds of people, laughing and chattering excitedly over their purchases.

Hardly anyone in the store seemed to notice the boy with the red-scarred face. Only the sales ladies eyed him sharply, knowing he was not there to buy. He jostled along with the multitude, letting his upturned face brush the back of a luxurious fur coat. The touch of soft fur and the scent of the lady wearing it dazzled him.

After that day, Roberto returned again and again to the grand store. He hid in the toy department to watch the well-dressed children. Their skin was smooth, their hair expertly cut at the best salons.

Most of all, Roberto admired the children with curly brown hair and skin like coffee with milk. That was what his mother drank each morning; each morning as he watched her drink it, he thought of these perfect children.

"Roberto of the Roses!
Roberto of the Roses!"

Roberto began to be bothered by the children who shouted at him in the street. Why did they never ask him to play with them? Was it simply because of his face?

Roberto blushed so red that the roses were almost hidden.

One summer evening Roberto was walking aimlessly through the streets of Barcelona, feeling sad and lonely. He turned down an unfamiliar street, when suddenly he gasped in wonder.

High on a hill above him stood a brightly lit palace. Below the palace played an enormous fountain, the largest he had ever seen.

The fountain was constantly changing, in the most mysterious way. While Roberto stood transfixed, it turned now as green as the northern lights, now as purple as a king's treasure.

Roberto stood in awe at the foot of the magical fountain. As he gazed upon that towering beauty, he felt all at once how ugly the mark on his face truly was.

He would have bowed his head in shame, except that the fountain drew his eyes upward to its sprays, flowering above him more gloriously than spring.

For the first time, he wanted with all the strength of his heart to be just like everyone else. He wished he could leap into the waters of the fountain and let their purples and greens and golds wash away his birthmark.

After that, Roberto of the Roses was no longer content to stay home on Saturday evenings, or to go out walking with his family. Instead, he returned each week to the fountain of lights. He would stand before it, feeling its spray on his face, letting its lights enchant him.

An old lady who sold yo-yos at the foot of the
fountain noticed the boy with the roses on his cheek.
She began to greet him whenever she saw him, and a
friendship grew up between the two. They shared much in
common, for she was old and hunched and not at all
lovely.

Saturday after Saturday Roberto would leave his home just after supper and venture forth into the dark streets. He had to go to the fountain. He was beginning to think of it as *his* fountain. He began to believe that the fountain had magical powers.

"If I just stand under it long enough," he said to himself, "it will make my skin like that of the others."

But every night he went sadly home, with the splotches standing out on his cheek just as before.

Every day he heard the same shouting from the others:

"Roberto of the Roses!
Roberto of the Roses!"

One evening, as Roberto stood spell bound beneath the brilliant waters, it came to him that he should ask the fountain for help. With the bright roses on his face, he felt like one of the poor parakeets, trapped in its wire cage. The magical fountain surely must have the power to set him free.

As he was thinking this, the hunchbacked yo-yo lady stopped and greeted him. Her beady eyes flashed in the changing light, and suddenly she spoke in a harsh tone as if she knew his thoughts:

"What you are doing is wrong—wrong! The fountain cannot help you. Go to the Master Artist! Go to the Master Artist!"

Then she hobbled off, calling out as before, "Yo-yos! Who will buy my yo-yos!"

Her words troubled Roberto, though he did not understand them. Who was this Master Artist? Did she mean the artist who had designed the fountain? And where would he find such an important person?

Roberto walked slowly around the circle of the fountain, his thoughts confused. On his second time around he noticed a man standing at an easel, painting a picture of the fountain.

An artist! If he were not the Master Artist, he might at least know where to find him.

Roberto came up behind the man and tugged gently at his sleeve.

"Please sir—are you the Master Artist?" he asked.

The man looked down. He had a kind, merry face, and he laughed a laugh that broke in the middle at the sight of Roberto's birthmark.

After a moment the man said quietly, "No. I am only an artist. There are many greater, and one who is greatest of all."

"I must find him," said Roberto. "Do you know where he is? I want so much not to be ugly any more."

At first the man looked astonished, but at last he laughed again, more merrily than before. He set down his paintbrush and took Roberto by the arm.

"Oh yes," he said, "I know this Master Artist. I can help you find him, and he will make you beautiful."

They began to stroll around the fountain. As they walked, the man told Roberto of the Master Artist. While he was talking, wonderful pictures came into Roberto's mind.

He pictured a world of dark nothingness, into which the Master Artist brought all the light and beauty of nature.

He pictured a world bursting forth green. The Master Artist spoke, and fish and birds and animals appeared, more and more until the earth was full.

He pictured the Master Artist making with loving care a man and a woman, to be master and mistress over his world.

But the most wonderful picture of all concerned the making of a certain boy who lived in Barcelona.

"Is it true?" asked Roberto with shining eyes, when he realized what this last picture meant. "Did the Master Artist really make me?"

The kind man nodded. "It's true," he said. "God the Creator made you, and he loves you very much. In his eyes you are beautiful just as you are—even with the roses on your face."

Roberto felt he would burst with joy. He began to dance and sing: "I am Roberto of the Roses! I am Roberto of the Roses!"

The passers-by stared with only a little astonishment, for things such as this could happen in Barcelona. The old lady grinned until her hooked nose and hooked chin almost touched each other.

The next day Roberto of the Roses was still dancing and singing. He danced down the street, calling proudly to the other children, "I am Roberto of the Roses! The Master Artist made me just like this. You're each different, too— have you noticed? That's because he made you that way!"

The children gaped in astonishment. Then they began to laugh and clap.

"Roberto of the Roses! Roberto of the Roses!" they shouted. "Come and play with us!"

And Roberto felt warm all the way down to his dancing toes.

AFTERWORD

Nearly all of us have something about ourselves that we don't like. Perhaps it is nothing as noticeable as the red roses on Roberto's cheek. On the other hand, it may be something quite obvious, which we think makes us different from other people. We may wish that we could change it, but we cannot.

God's heart is so big that he sees everyone in his creation as beautiful. Each of us has great value in his eyes. Roberto learned to like himself when he saw that God loves him exactly as he is.

Wouldn't it be boring if we were all merely copies of one another? Let's enjoy being one of a kind—one of the Master Artist's special creations!

If you happen to be in Barcelona, and visit the National Palace on Montjuich on certain evenings, you can see Roberto's magical fountain.

Text copyright © 1988 Donna Reid Vann
Illustrations copyright © 1988 John Haysom

The author asserts the moral right
to be identified as the author of this work

Published by
Lion Publishing plc
Sandy Lane West, Oxford, England
ISBN 0 7459 2258 9
Albatross Books Pty Ltd
PO Box 320, Sutherland, NSW 2232, Australia
ISBN 0 7324 0681 1

First edition 1988
First paperback edition 1993

A catalogue record for this book is available
from the British Library

Printed and bound in Singapore

Other picture storybooks in paperback from Lion Publishing

Albert Blows A Fuse Tom Bower

Baboushka Arthur Scholey

The Donkey's Day Out Ann Pilling

John Porter in Big Trouble Tim Stafford

The Lark who had no Song Carolyn Nystrom

A Lion for the King Meryl Doney

Mabel and the Tower of Babel John Ryan

Papa Panov's Special Day Mig Holder

Stefan's Secret Fear Donna Reid Vann

The Tale of Three Trees Angela Elwell Hunt

The Very Worried Sparrow Meryl Doney